DANGER ZONE:
Dieting and Eating Disorders™

DIET FADS

Barbara A. Zahensky

ROSEN
PUBLISHING®

New York

Published in 2007 by The Rosen Publishing Group, Inc.
29 East 21st Street, New York, NY 10010

First Edition

Library of Congress Cataloging-in-Publication Data

Zahensky, Barbara A.
Diet fads / Barbara A. Zahensky.
    p. cm.—(Danger zone. Dieting and eating disorders)
Includes bibliographical references.
ISBN-13: 978-1-4042-1999-1
ISBN-10: 1-4042-1999-4 (library binding)
1. Reducing diets—Juvenile literature. 2. Weight loss—
Juvenile literature. 3. Obesity—Prevention—Juvenile
literature. I. Title.
RM222.2.Z34 2006
613.2'5—dc22

                                              2006032245

Manufactured in the United States of America

Contents

1

Your Weight and Body

Do you or others you know want to be thinner? Do you go on and off different diets trying to find one that will work for you? In the United States today, many young people believe that they have to be thin to be attractive. Fashion magazines and popular television shows feature very slim models and actors.

This idea about having a model's body, along with the pressure from other teens, makes many young people feel that they must be thin. Sometimes this quest for thinness can lead to serious health problems. According to the National Eating Disorders Association, it is estimated that in 2005, as many as ten million females and one million males in the United States suffered from an eating disorder such as anorexia nervosa or bulimia nervosa. Furthermore,

Superskinny celebrities, like Nicole Richie *(top)*, and fashion models are believed to provide "thinspiration" to young women who diet to reach an extreme ideal of thinness.

about twenty-five million more people were fighting a battle with binge eating disorder. According to the Eating Disorders Coalition, an organization that works to advance federal recognition of eating disorders as a top priority in public health, 90 percent of those suffering from an eating disorder are adolescent and young women. In general,

To cater to weight-conscious diners, national restaurant chains have recently added diet items to their menus. You can easily prepare a more healthful meal at home, however.

however, the statistics on eating disorders are somewhat inaccurate because of the secretiveness of those with disordered eating behaviors and because doctors are not required to report eating disorders.

At the same time that extreme thinness has become so desirable in American society today, the average teen has become less active physically than in past generations. Most young people spend much more time watching television or playing video games. They drive or ride in a car rather than walk or bike to wherever they need to go. Many teens do not participate in any regular exercise program or team sport either at school or at home.

DIETS

When you don't burn calories with exercise, the only way
to reduce weight is to eat less. As a result, countless articles
and books have been written about dieting, and thousands
of weight-loss centers (such as Weight Watchers, Jenny
Craig, and NutriSystem) have been established across the
United States to offer people methods or programs for losing weight.

Diets based on good nutrition can be very helpful. And
some well-established weight loss plans are staffed by
experts on health and nutrition and can be a source of support and help if you want to lose weight. But many are
crash or fad diets, which are not only unhealthy, but can be
dangerous. A fad diet is a diet that is a craze or in fashion,
that is, it is followed with great enthusiasm by a lot of
people for a short period of time. Fad diets focus on losing
a lot of weight quickly. They are not usually created by
experts in nutrition, but by people or companies who are
only interested in making a quick dollar. They rely on
people's insecurity and negative feelings about themselves
to sell ineffective diet books, prepared meals, or products
for "instant weight loss." These diets can injure your health

and cause serious problems. If the diet seems too good to be true, for example, if it offers a significant weight loss by your eating only cookies or only food that is white in color, or weight loss while you are sleeping, it probably isn't a healthy one. You'll need to use common sense when you are considering diet possibilities.

It is important to learn ways to feel good about yourself and your body, how to eat only when you are hungry, and how to develop habits that will help you keep your weight under control for the rest of your life.

SELF-ESTEEM

Many young people feel that losing weight will solve their problems. They think that once they lose weight, they will be accepted and make friends easily. These teens have a problem with low self-esteem. Self-esteem is how you feel about yourself. It is the feeling that you are likeable just the way you are. With high self-esteem you feel worthwhile, no matter how you look.

There are certain times in life when self-esteem is more likely to be low. Adolescence can be one of those times. Adolescence is a time of many changes. It's common for teens to wonder if they are ready to grow up.

It's typical to worry about how you look and what your peers think of you.

It's also natural to feel negative about yourself every so often. Just remember that there are many things you can do to help yourself feel better. If you are overweight, that's nothing to be ashamed of. Weight problems are not easy to handle. You need to find someone who can help you plan the safest way to lose your unwanted pounds. Understanding more about your weight problem may also help you feel better about yourself.

WHAT IS FAT?

Being fat means different things to different people. When

Oftentimes, fatness is in the eye of the beholder. A recent survey of over 2,000 respondents revealed that nine out of ten people believe that the majority of other Americans are fat.

someone says, "I'm fat," it could mean one of the following three things:

1. The person is obese. A person who is obese has an excess amount of body fat. Many medical experts consider a female who has 30 percent more body fat than the average female, who has between 25 and 30 percent of body fat, to be obese. A male is considered to be obese if his body fat is more that 25 percent (an average male has between 18 and 23 percent of body fat).

2. The person is overweight. Someone who is over-weight is somewhat heavier than an average person of the same age and build.

3. The person "feels" fatter than he or she wants to be, even though his or her weight falls within a healthy range.

"Fat" also has another meaning. It is one of the three major components of the food you eat. The other two are carbohydrates and proteins.

Fats come from milk products, meats, fish, nuts, and veg-etable oils, as well as many packaged foods like chips and candy bars. There is almost all fat in butter and margarine.

Carbohydrates (also called carbs) come from fruits, sugars, and foods made from flour (bread, pasta, and crackers). Carbohydrates are the class of foods that supply energy to your body. Carbohydrates are also found in rice, corn, potatoes, and other vegetables. Protein is found in meat, fish, chicken, eggs, cheese, nuts and beans, and vegetables. Proteins are vital to the formation and activity of all living things.

BODY FAT IS NECESSARY

Fats are stored in cells called adipocytes. "Adipo" means fat. "Cyte" means cell. Adipocytes cushion your organs and bones. They protect you from cold.

Fat cells also store energy. Energy is the ability of the body to do its work. Your body needs energy to grow. Energy makes your heart beat. It helps you blink your eyes and move your arms and legs.

You get energy from the foods you eat. Calories measure the amount of energy that each food produces when it is burned up by the body. If you eat more calories than you burn up, you gain weight. The excess weight is stored as fat.

Everyone is born with fat cells. Some people have too many. Extra cells develop during infancy and childhood. Some also develop during the teenage years. Once you stop growing, no new fat cells are added.

Myths and Facts About Diet Fads

Myth: I can eat all I want because when I want to lose weight, I can just go on a crash diet.

Fact: Fad diets focus on losing a lot of weight in a short time. They are not created by experts in nutrition, but usually by people or companies who are only interested in making a quick dollar. They rely on people's insecurity and negative feelings about themselves to sell ineffective diet books or products for "instant weight loss." These diets can injure your health and cause serious problems.

Myth: Natural or herbal products for losing weight are safe and effective.

Fact: These types of weight-loss products are not always safe. Generally, the products have not been scientifically tested to prove that they are healthy or that they work. Herbal products that contain ephedra are now banned by the federal government because they were found to cause serious health problems and even death in some people who took them. Furthermore, products that claim to be ephedra-free are not necessarily safe because they could contain ingredients that are similar to ephedra.

Myth: If I skip breakfast or lunch, I will lose weight faster.

Fact: If you eat fewer meals you can gain weight and body fat eventually. By eating fewer meals, your body fights back by decreasing the rate at which you burn calories. Most experts suggest that you can lose weight more effectively if you eat several small meals each day rather than one or two large meals.

Myth: Low-fat or fat-free food means that there are no calories in the food.

Fact: A food that is called low-fat or fat-free is often lower in calories than a full-fat food that is the same size portion. However, many processed low-fat or fat-free foods can have the same number or more of calories as the full-fat type of the food. These low-fat or fat-free foods can contain added sugar, flour, or starch thickeners that have been added to improve the texture and the way the food tastes after the fat has been removed. These extra ingredients add calories.

Myth: Just because I am on a fad diet now doesn't mean that I'll need to be on one again.

Fact: According to the National Eating Disorders Association, about 35 percent of average dieters move on to become people who diet excessively, and, of those about 20 percent develop an eating disorder.

Once cells are added, they won't go away. But diet and exercise can help. Diet and exercise will not lower the total number of fat cells, but they can make each cell give up some of its fat and get smaller.

YOUR BODY'S METABOLISM

Have you ever known people who can eat as much as they like but never gain weight? Perhaps you are one of those people. There are definitely differences in the way people burn their food. The amount of food it takes to give the body the energy it uses depends on the metabolism.

For example, Sharyl and Tamara are both fifteen and about 5'3" tall. They both attend the same classes and take aerobics together after school. They both eat a peanut butter and jelly sandwich for lunch every day. Yet Sharyl has a weight problem and Tamara doesn't. This is because Sharyl and Tamara do not have the same metabolism, and their bodies operate differently. Tamara never stops moving. She is always twirling a pen or moving her feet. These extra body movements may burn up more of her calories. Sharyl eats a doughnut or coffee cake in the morning, and has dessert after dinner. Tamara doesn't. These extra calories often add up to extra pounds. Sharyl's dad is overweight. Her mom has a large bone structure and is stocky. Tamara's parents are of average weight. Some researchers believe that the tendency to be fat can be passed on. They have found that an overweight child usually has at least one overweight parent. Some say that this shows that obesity is passed along the genes. But other researchers disagree. They say that parents and children who are overweight share the same poor eating habits. The overweight parent and child may also be relatively inactive. Both eating and activity patterns affect a family's weight.

Does your family eat small, lean meals and exercise regularly? Then you will probably not have a weight problem. If your family has not taught you good eating habits, you can learn them on your own.

HOW MUCH SHOULD I WEIGH?

You've probably seen charts giving the average height and weight for people of your age and sex. Remember that these figures are an average. Each person's "normal weight" or set-point differs. Your weight depends on your bone structure. It also depends on how much muscle development you have. You can actually be "overweight" on a chart without being fat. Take Les, for example. Les is a wrestler. He's developed lots of muscles. Muscle tissue is heavier than fat. If Les paid attention to the weight charts, he might think he's overweight. But he's not.

There are several ways doctors or registered dietitians can measure body fat. A common, accurate method uses a special tool called a skin-fold caliper. The caliper gently squeezes and measures a fold of skin. Good places to measure are on the back and the upper arm. A thicker skin fold means more fat. Another way to measure how much body fat a person has is by using a formula called the body mass index, or BMI. The BMI formula uses a person's height and weight measurements to compute a BMI number. Calculating the BMI for teens is different from figuring it out for adults because not all teens have the same body build or develop at the same time.

If you've been overweight since you were young, you probably carry around too many fat cells. Don't be discouraged. You can keep your weight down by keeping the level of fat in your cells low. But you can't keep your fat level low by fad dieting. Fad diets promote losing weight too quickly. You cannot stay on such a diet for a long time. As soon as you stop a fad diet, your "greedy" cells will grab onto all the extra calories your regular diet supplies. You'll gain back all the weight you lost—and fast! Forbes.com reported in September 2006 that according to a government survey, two-thirds of Americans who dieted regained all the weight they had lost within one year, and 97 percent had gained all of it back within five years.

The best way to keep your weight down is to learn how to make wise food choices. Learn how to cook low-fat meals. Learn how to enjoy healthy meals. Get in the habit of exercising. Then you will burn up calories before they are stored as fat.

2

Why Some People Overeat

American society is not very friendly toward people who are overweight. They do not understand that in most cases the person has not chosen to be overweight. Being overweight does not always come from overeating alone—metabolism has a lot to do with it. However, many people are unable to stop themselves from overeating.

If you are one of those people, you have nothing to be ashamed of. It does not make you weak or a failure. It may mean that you are unhappy; for example, you may eat a chocolate bar every time you get depressed. Or you may be a compulsive eater (also called a binge eater). This is a person who cannot resist eating, and he or she eats a lot of food often. Sometimes feelings deep inside the person forces a compulsive eater to overeat. The problem is that compulsive

On television and in advertisements, the pressure to be thin coexists with the temptation of food. Such mixed messages can lead to binge-ing and other eating disorders.

eaters don't always eat because they are hungry—they often feel out of control and unable to stop eating even when they should feel full. This eating disorder, called binge eating disor-der, is a serious condition. About 5 percent of males suffer from binge eating disorder, according to the Eating Disorders Coalition. Certain risk factors for this eating disorder can include a genetic predisposition, or familial or peer problems (such as physical, emotional, or sexual abuse).

Sometimes people overeat just to have something to do with their hands. Snacking is common while watching television or a movie. Some other reasons why people eat more than they should are:

- to reward themselves
- to please others
- to avoid waste, especially at restaurants

WHAT YOU LEARNED AS A CHILD

For most people, eating is also a social function. Babies first experience loving human contact through eating. They are cuddled and comforted when they eat. Many children never lose this feeling that food is soothing, even after they have grown up. Mealtimes can be a time for family sharing. Parties and holiday celebrations are often arranged around food and its preparation. It's easy to overeat when so many of your favorite foods are served.

For some children, eating may be a way to deal with their problems. Have you ever "pigged out" because you felt sad, depressed, lonely, nervous, or angry? Usually, eating can make you feel better for a time. However, it doesn't help you to understand what caused the negative feelings. In fact, overeating may actually cause another problem: guilt.

Some teens get caught in a cycle of overeating, which is very difficult to break. Being overweight makes them depressed, but eating makes them feel better. When they have finished eating, they feel guilty. Most young people are critical of themselves. This is how a negative cycle grows.

UNDER PRESSURE

There are many different reasons why you may be unhappy with the way you look, especially with the way your body looks. Some of these reasons are not always obvious. For example, your parents may make you feel as though you "aren't good enough." They may be very critical and push you constantly to be better, which causes you to want to be thinner. Perhaps you feel that your being more attractive will please them and take some of the pressure off of you.

You may also feel pressure from friends or relatives who criticize you or say you should be more like somebody else. Or maybe you compare yourself to others too often. You put yourself down for not being as popular or attractive as they are.

This kind of judging and comparing goes on all the time. No one person can truly judge another. Who's to say what's really "attractive" or "the best"? It's hard to fight off critical feelings if you don't feel good about your body. Your body image is how satisfied you are with your size and shape. It is changeable. When you're feeling up, your body image is great. When you're feeling down, your body image will most likely be low.

You probably have in your mind a picture of the perfect body. You know just how you would look if you could make yourself over. These ideas come mainly from the following three places:

- your peers
- your parents
- the media (television, newspapers, magazines and e-zines, and movies)

Each group has their own opinions about how you should look. Usually the message is that being thin is fashionable and healthy.

WHAT SOCIETY HAS TO SAY

Thin hasn't always been in. Look at a painting by the Flemish artist Peter Paul Rubens, or the Italian master Titian. Most of the people painted in their works are shown as being plump.

Why Some People Overeat

The women are full-figured (in fact, this is where the term "Rubenesque," meaning plump or rounded, comes from). In American society around the 1900s, plump, curvy women were also thought to be more attractive than thin women.

Even now, in some cultures, fat is greatly respected. Japanese sumo wrestlers are highly honored. They are huge men who must continually overeat to maintain their size. In many developing countries, people want to be plump. This is a sign of wealth. They are proud to be able to afford as much food as they want.

Today in the United States, however, fat is considered ugly. Overeating is considered unwise, unhealthy, and sometimes

Many celebrities, such as Lindsay Lohan, have dramatically slimmed down in the public eye. This can add to the pressure to go on crash diets and quickly drop the pounds.

unforgivable. You can see this "ideal" in some popular American role models. It seems as though everybody on TV or in movies has a perfect body. For example, look at the influence such actors as Leonardo DiCaprio and Colin Farrell, or Lindsay Lohan and Jessica Biel have on young people regarding body image and appearance. When Oprah Winfrey and Janet Jackson lost weight, the entire country talked about how great they looked.

There are a few stars who break the mold, like Queen Latifah and Jack Black, but most of the messages you get from the media insist that it is better to be thin. It is true that losing weight and getting into shape can often make you feel better about yourself. But you should be aware of who is causing you to become thinner. Is it truly your own desire, or are you doing it because you feel pressure from others?

3

No Easy Solution

Give us a week, we'll take off the weight!" "How to look your best in ten easy steps!" "Lose weight without ever feeling hungry!" These are the kinds of ads that surround us in today's fashion magazines, on television, and on the Internet. According to some medical researchers, Americans spend more than $40 billion each year on dieting and diet-related products. But the truth is that nobody should have to spend any money at all to lose fat. As an individual, you need to create your own personal weight loss plan. This should include what and how much you eat, an exercise routine, and most important, a positive attitude and outlook.

   With any weight reduction program it's hard to keep the weight off. As reported by the National Eating Disorders

Association, about 25 percent of American males and 45 percent of American females are on a diet on any given day and most of them will gain back any weight they lost in one to five years. The body is used to processing food for a fatter person. Dieters often find themselves slipping back to their old eating habits. The result is a "yo-yo" effect. A lot of weight is lost fast. But a lot of weight is gained back quickly. The person feels guilty and starts a new diet. The yo-yo cycle continues.

Such a cycle of gaining and losing weight is dangerous. It's more of a strain on the body than staying at one level, even an overweight level. Yo-yo dieting tends to raise the fat and cholesterol levels in the blood, which increases the risk of heart disease.

FASTING

Fasting is a time when a person does not eat, or eats very little. Sometimes people fast for religious purposes. But this is usually for a short time, a few hours or a single day. Fasting for longer periods of time is not a healthy way to lose weight. It deprives your body of important minerals known as electrolytes. Electrolytes send an electrical message that causes the heart to beat correctly. By fasting, you may develop dangerous heart problems even if you do not have a history of heart trouble.

ONE-FOOD DIETS

There are some fad diets where you are asked to eat mostly one type of food, such as the grapefruit diet or the cabbage soup diet. The grapefruit diet (a twelve-day plan) involves eating one-half grapefruit or drinking grapefruit juice at every meal, which could also include boiled eggs and dry toast. Proponents of this kind of diet believe that the grapefruit compounds lower insulin levels, which can then help in reducing weight. The cabbage soup diet, where dieters eat cabbage soup for seven days, is supplemented by another food on each day of the diet. Critics of this fad diet believe that the weight loss comes mainly from the loss of water in the body and the huge calorie restriction, and not from any fat-burning benefits. One-food diets such as these, where calories can be too restrictive, can cause blood pressure and heart problems if they are continued for longer periods of time.

LOW-CARBOHYDRATE DIETS

Low-carb diets are based on eating few carbohydrates (breads, starches, and pasta). Instead of the high-energy

Diet fads come and go, and the sudden appearance of low-carb snacks on grocery shelves shows that food manufacturers aim to cash in on the latest dieting trends.

foods, the dieter eats lots of eggs, meat, chicken, fish, cheese, and other high-protein foods. Too much protein may overtax the kidneys, eventually leading to kidney failure. These foods are also high in fats and cholesterol that can lead to heart problems in some people. Other side effects of a low-carbohydrate diet may be:

- bad breath
- headaches
- fainting
- dehydration (losing too much water)
- cravings for carbohydrates, especially candy

28

LIQUID DIETS

Most liquid diets suggest a diet drink for two meals. Only one meal allows solid food. Special foods may be part of the diet plan, too.

Many people have success with liquid diets—at first. But it's hard to live on diet drinks for long periods of time. Once off the liquid diet, the dieter doesn't know how to make sensible meal choices. It is easy to go back to the old eating habits and regain the lost weight.

Liquid diet programs can be expensive. Most of these programs are supposed to be done with the help of a doctor or other health professional. Teens who go on liquid diets tend to buy the liquid products at drug stores. They don't check with their doctor or a nutritionist first. Many teens use the products incorrectly and suffer side effects, including the following:

- nausea
- dizziness
- extreme fatigue
- hair loss
- irritability
- irregular menstruation (periods)

DIET PILLS

The most powerful diet pills available contain amphetamines. Amphetamines must be prescribed by a doctor. These drugs "pep up" the body and decrease appetite. They work for only a short time and are very dangerous if used incorrectly. Large amounts of amphetamines over time may cause permanent brain damage, extreme fatigue, and even death.

Other diet pills are sold without a doctor's prescription. They are well advertised on television and at drug stores. Many of these pills use sugar to control appetite. Nevertheless, the sugar adds extra calories.

Some diet pills are diuretics (drugs that make the body lose water). Diuretics don't make you lose fat. They can be dangerous if misused, because the body needs water to remain healthy.

LAXATIVES

Drugs that cause bowel movements are known as laxatives. Sometimes dieters use them to rid, or purge, the body of unwanted food. However, many important vitamins and minerals can also be lost this way.

Overuse of laxatives can cause stomach pain, cramps, diarrhea, and extreme fatigue. The body has no energy left to function.

Laxatives should be used only for occasional irregularity. If you use laxatives to lose weight, your body will begin to depend on them. Once you stop using them, it may be nearly impossible to have a bowel movement normally.

HEALTH FOODS

Foods promoted as "health," "natural," or "whole" foods may not necessarily be wise diet choices. Oatmeal muffins contain oat bran, a good source of fiber. But many muffins have more calories and fat than cream-filled doughnuts. Some fruit-filled yogurts can be high in sugar. Check the labels of the foods you buy. It is important to know what you are eating even if you are not on a diet.

IS A VEGETARIAN DIET HEALTHY?

Some people decide to become vegetarians because they believe in animal rights and feel that eating meat is cruel. Others believe that eliminating meat from their diet will help them to lose weight. Some people go even one step further and follow a vegan diet, which is a vegetarian diet that does not include any animal products, including eggs and dairy products. Both vegetarian and vegan diets require a balance of important vitamins and minerals to be healthy diets.

Young people need plenty of protein and calcium to grow properly. If you choose a vegetarian or vegan diet you should include some dairy products, legumes (such as soybeans), nuts, grains, fruits, and berries. A diet without these food groups depletes the body of vitamin B12, which can result in diarrhea, skin problems, and mental confusion. If you are a vegetarian and are limiting your calories to lose weight, consider taking a multivitamin.

DESIGNING A HEALTHY PLAN

Check with your doctor and your parents before starting any diet. Registered dietitians and nutritionists recommend losing no more than one-half to two pounds each week because rapid weight loss can be unhealthy. You don't want your body to be malnourished. A sensible diet should include:

- a variety of nutritious foods
- sufficient protein
- enough carbohydrates (breads and pasta)
- lots of vegetables and fruits
- small amounts of fat (butter, oils, fatty meats)
- few high-calorie items (candy and desserts)

No Easy Solution

You don't need to take on too rigid a diet. If it's too tough, you probably won't follow it for long. It is best to have a long-term plan for weight loss that you can live with.

You can avoid diets that require you to buy many special products. Pre-packaged diet foods are expensive. It is possible to lose weight and stay healthy by eating foods that you prepare yourself. You need to do some meal planning before you shop. And you should try to buy only what you need for your plan at the supermarket. Then you won't be tempted to grab the foods that are low in nutritional content at home when you are hungry.

An informed diet plan not only gives you more food options, such as fresh produce, it also increases your likelihood of meeting your diet goals and sustaining your ideal weight.

A DIET SUMMARY

A good diet is based on healthy eating habits. Once you've lost your desired amount of weight, you should continue with the same healthy eating habits. Then the weight lost will most likely stay off.

Fad diets over a period of time are clearly dangerous. They harm both the body and the mind. They can lead to life-threatening eating disorders such as anorexia and bulimia. Avoid any diet that promises a large weight loss in a short time. It is important to break the cycle of overeating and develop your own plan for healthy eating.

What Is Hunger?

Certain activities and feelings lead to food choices that are based on habit, not hunger. For some, coming home from school means they next get to eat a sweet snack. For others, going to a friend's house means it's time for munchies. Watching television can be a signal to bring out the ice cream. People with weight problems often make these kinds of choices—almost without thinking.

Television ads may foster bad eating habits. Food is shown and talked about so much that it can make you feel everyone else is eating and having fun. You join in, many times, even though you aren't hungry.

It's OK to have snacks on occasion. And it's great to enjoy good food in the company of friends. The problem is that too often you eat without thinking. You need to be aware of why you are eating.

If you're overweight, think of how you are feeling when you have the desire to eat. If you cannot control your food intake, you may need help for some emotional problem. In time it may feel more natural to choose non-eating activities when you are upset. You'll be on your way to developing new, healthier habits.

WHY DO YOU EAT?

Do you eat when you are afraid or lonely? Do you eat when you are frustrated? Do you tell yourself, "I'm so fat. I might as well go ahead and eat. What difference does it make?" Once you understand your reasons for eating, you'll be better able to control your eating. Here's a plan to help you get started:

1. **Write down your reasons for overeating.** Be honest with yourself. Do this in a quiet place. What you write is private.

2. **Write down your reasons for wanting to lose weight.** Look closely at what you've written. Are these your reasons? Or have you written down what you think others expect of you?

3. **Write down what makes you feel good about yourself.** There is something about you that makes you special. These thoughts will help you feel up when you're tempted to overeat.

4. **Make an eating chart.** Write down everything you eat for each meal and snack. Also include the following information:

- when you eat
- where you eat
- whom you eat with
- how you feel at the time (sad, happy, lonely, celebrating, etc.)
- how hungry you are (not, little, starving)

Keep this chart for two weeks. With it, you can learn many things about yourself. It will show you when you make eating choices based on feelings, instead of true hunger.

LEARN TO RECOGNIZE HUNGER

Your stomach and brain give you signals about when and how much to eat. The signals are related to your blood sugar levels. Blood sugar carries fuel to the cells. It stays at a certain level a few hours after a meal. When you eat something sweet, your blood sugar level rises. It also rises after a large meal. It drops during exercise and activity. As it drops, your stomach may growl. This is a sign of hunger.

For each person, blood sugar enters the muscles at a different rate. The rate depends on how active you are and how much body fat you have. You probably know thin people who always seem to be snacking. Yet they never gain weight. They eat just enough food to satisfy their hunger. Their blood sugar stays at about the same level all the time.

Let's look at what can happen to blood sugar levels during a typical day. This will help you understand how to recognize true hunger pangs.

Choosing to diet should be a positive choice and free of the pressures to lose a certain amount of weight by a deadline or meet other unrealistic goals.

What Is Hunger?

When you get up in the morning, your blood sugar level depends on what you ate the night before. If you ate half a pizza at midnight, you may not feel hungry right away. As you rush about getting ready for the day, you use up a lot of blood sugar. You'll start to feel hungry. If you don't eat, you may get a headache. You may even feel faint, dizzy, or sick to your stomach.

If you ignore these hunger signals, your blood sugar will remain low. Your body will slow down to save energy. You may begin to feel sleepy and find it hard to concentrate.

Your liver will then send signals to increase your blood sugar level. Suddenly, you'll pep up. Lots of people think this means they don't need to eat during the day. Some people trick their bodies into getting this full feeling. This is done by drinking beverages that contain caffeine such as coffee, tea, or soda.

Going without food or living on caffeine is a strain on your system. Your body may think it is "starving" so when you finally eat, your body holds on to more of the calories. It won't use up any of your stored fat.

There is another problem with trying to go without food. By the end of the day, you're starving. Studies have shown that people who wait all day to eat actually eat more in 24 hours because their hunger is so huge. In fact, some people who skip a meal end up eating twice as much at the next meal.

If you want to lose weight, listen to your body. Pay attention to your blood sugar signals. If your stomach is growling, eat something healthy. Try some fruit and cheese. Avoid sugary foods with "empty calories" that will send your blood sugar level up fast and high, but not for long. When it drops back down again, you may feel even hungrier than before. It is always better to choose healthy foods that will satisfy your hunger longer, because you will probably end up eating less in the long run.

5

Positive Planning

You probably have a mental picture of yourself. It is made up of the thoughts you tell yourself over and over. Often these thoughts are negative. For example, you may tell yourself: "I'm fat and unattractive." "I can't change." "I've got no willpower." "I'll never be thin, I've got big bones."

If you think negative thoughts long enough, you can be trapped into believing them. But you can break out of this trap. Think ahead to what you want to be. Form a new picture of yourself in your mind. A positive self-image may help you to reach your goals for self-improvement.

Be realistic. You won't be able to make all the changes at once.

Write down your own goals on a "New Me" form. Complete the following statements:

Danger Zone: Diet Fads

- My goal weight is_____.
- To reach my goal weight I will change my eating habits by not_____.
- At my new weight, I will try to do these things differently: _____.
- If I stray from my diet plan sometimes, I will

  _____.

Often, our most negative thoughts are about dieting itself. Think about the advertising you may have heard for diet plans. Maybe they promise things such as the following:

- Lose 50 pounds fast!
- The more weight you lose, the better you'll feel!
- Don't eat all weekend and feel great!
- You only need one meal a day!

These diet statements are unhealthy and dangerous. They are also hard to achieve. Plan a healthy diet that is manageable. Remember that no one is perfect. On some meals, you will "cheat" a little. That's natural. Think about what you've done right with your diet, instead of what you couldn't resist. At bedtime each evening, remind yourself that you did your best and tomorrow you can do even better.

CALORIE COUNT

Think positively about what you can eat instead of what you can't. Calories are only a problem if you take in more than you burn up. There are recommended amounts of calories for you to eat each day, but this number depends on how old you are, whether or not you are active, and whether you are trying to gain weight, lose weight, or maintain weight. To learn more about what amount of calories may be healthy for you, go to the U.S. Department of Agriculture's Web site, which provides information on the dietary guidelines for Americans (http://www.health.gov).

REDUCING FAT

Limiting fat in your diet is one of the best ways to improve your health and to lose weight. However, you should not reduce your fat intake to less than 30 percent of your calorie intake. One fad diet suggested eating as much as you want, as long as no more than 10 percent of the calories you ate came from fat. But most experts agree this number is too low. Cutting your fat intake to 10 percent could keep your body from growing properly and could prevent you from getting the nutrients you need to be healthy. If just under one-third of the calories you need daily come from fat, you should be able to lose weight without losing your health.

There are different kinds of fats in different foods. In general, animal fats are not as desirable as vegetable fats. For almost any food product you buy, information about fat, calories, and cholesterol is listed on the package's ingredients label along with other nutritional data.

PLANNING A LIFELONG DIET

If you are very active or still growing, you'll need to allow for more calories in your diet. Ask your doctor or registered dietitian or nutritionist for more information on food groups and calorie counts for specific foods in each category. Then you can keep track of your daily calories and adjust your number of servings.

To help you keep track of your allowed foods, draw a daily chart. After each meal, check off what you have eaten. Another way is to cut strips of paper. Write each allowed food on a strip. Store the strips on one side of a notebook. As you eat the food, move the strip for that food to the other side of the notebook. By the end of the day, you should have moved all your strips to the other side.

WATCH OUT FOR HIDDEN CALORIES

Most people think of a salad as a low-calorie meal. Salads can be a healthy diet choice with some exceptions. Watch out for the high-fat, high-calorie extras. Avoid too much cheese, avocado, bacon bits, and fatty dressings. You can eat as much lettuce, cucumber, celery, onions, mushrooms, and alfalfa sprouts as you want. These veggies have virtually no calories.

How much soda do you drink daily? Soda contains no vitamins or minerals necessary for good health. But a 12-ounce can of regular soda has 9 teaspoons of sugar and approximately 120 calories. If you drink one can per day, those extra calories could cause a 10-pound (4.5-kilogram) weight gain in only one year! Sometimes so-called sugar-free soda contains corn syrup or other sweeteners. Read the labels to make sure you're getting a true low-calorie product. It is important to drink a lot of fluids each day. Water is always the best choice—it's calorie-free and essential for your body to function. Other ideas would include vegetable juice or low-fat or non-fat (skim) milk.

6

Diet Tips for Good Eating Habits

Deciding to make healthy food choices is easier said than done, but it's worth it. As you learn new eating habits and lose weight, your self-image will change. You'll feel better about yourself. Some practical hints for success include the following:

1. **When you're tempted to snack, do something active.** Get up and go for a walk. (Do not walk to the refrigerator!) Call a friend. Write a letter. Do some yard work. Research has shown that the urge to eat usually dies down after twenty minutes. Try to keep busy for at least twenty minutes. A drink of water may be enough to satisfy you after that.

2. **Make an emergency box to keep in the refrigerator.** Fill it with carrots, celery, broccoli,

Eating sensibly, exercising regularly, and getting support from your family and friends are three important factors in dieting the right way.

green peppers, and tomatoes. When you get the irresistible urge to snack, head for your emergency box instead of a candy box!

3. **Change your eating style.** Chew more slowly. Be sure to swallow between each bite. Put your fork or spoon down between bites. These suggestions sound

obvious. But think about them during your next meal. Check to see if you're gulping down your food. If you are, slow down and taste your food. Eating with others can also help. If you stop to talk or listen during meals, you will naturally eat more slowly.

When you're eating, just eat. Don't read. Don't talk on the phone. Don't watch TV. Concentrate on the textures and smells of what you're eating. Take the time to enjoy each meal and snack.

4. **Quit the "clean plate" club.** Leave a little bit on your plate at the end of each meal. You may have to persuade your family to allow this. Explain that you're trying to break yourself of the habit of overeating. What also helps is to serve yourself smaller portions or use a smaller plate.

5. **Get rid of temptation.** Have you got cookies stashed in your desk drawer? Does your family have a candy dish in almost every room? What goodies are in the back seat of the car? Ask your family's help in keeping all food in the kitchen only.

6. **Plan snacks and meals.** Planning your meals will help you stay on track. Begin with one meal at a time. For example, set limits before going to a restaurant. Tell yourself the following:

"I can drink water instead of a soft drink."

"I will avoid high-fat foods."

"I'll have fruit at home for my dessert."

Thinking through choices ahead of time will help you avoid the temptation to overeat. This is especially important when you're going out with friends.

7. **Avoid the high-fat trend.** Americans seem to love high-fat cooking. The typical American diet often consists of foods fried in butter or lard, red meats, gravies, cream sauces, cheeses, and rich desserts. The number of people who are obese in the United States has doubled in the past two decades. Nearly one-third of adults are obese and it is estimated that 16 percent of children and adolescents are overweight.

Many people working in the nutrition industry have noticed a trend moving away from fitness and back to high-fat indulgence. To help you avoid being swept along with this unhealthy development, follow these recommendations:

- Use skim or reduced-fat milk
- Make macaroni and cheese without the butter or margarine

- Take advantage of low-fat and nonfat products that are available at most grocery stores.
- Avoid fried foods

8. **Use your scale wisely.** Don't weigh yourself every day. It's too soon to see any changes. Instead, weigh yourself once every week at the same time of the day. Even better, take notice of how your clothes are fitting. If they are getting tighter, you may be gaining weight. Or if they feel looser, you are losing those unwanted pounds. Keep it up!

9. **Reward yourself!** If you've reached your goal for the week, treat yourself to something special. Go to a movie. Buy a new book. Praise yourself for doing well.

   One of the best rewards for people watching their weight is food. Pick a favorite food. Allow yourself a reasonable amount of it. You'll have this reward to look forward to for each week of dieting. For example, a scoop of your favorite ice cream makes a great reward. But make it a single scoop!

10. **Add exercise.** Your natural weight is a kind of balance between the daily calories taken in and the calories used up. To reduce weight, a body needs to burn up more calories than it takes in.

Diet Tips for Good Eating Habits

Researchers have found that total weight loss is greater and healthier when dieters exercise. The more you move, the more calories you burn. Therefore, the more you exercise, the more you can eat. Think of the variety of foods you can enjoy—maybe even dessert once in a while. With regular exercise, your appetite will decrease. Exercise also helps your body use food more efficiently.

Getting exercise is not just about burning calories and losing weight. More important, it's about being the healthiest you can be and even having some fun.

Ten Great Questions to Ask When You're Asking for Help

1. What is an appropriate weight for my height?

2. How can I lose weight safely?

3. If I want to diet to lose weight, do I have to be under a doctor's care while I am dieting?

4. Do I have to exercise to lose weight?

5. Which is more important for my weight control, careful eating habits or an increase in exercise?

6. If I exercise regularly, do I still need to pay attention to good nutrition?

7. How much weight should I lose each week until I reach my goal?

8. How come some people can eat fattening foods and they don't seem to gain weight?

9. If I lose weight too fast, will I develop an eating disorder?

10. Because I am overweight now, will I always struggle with my weight?

EXERCISE IS FOR EVERYONE

It might seem as though most types of exercise today are done outdoors. Some of the most popular aerobic activities are in-line skating, jogging or speed walking, and cross-country skiing. If you are uncomfortable exercising in public, or if you are not accustomed to physical activity, you can still develop a successful exercise program at home.

You should not dread starting an exercise program. Think of it as something positive you are doing for yourself. Eventually you will look forward to your workouts, and you may find that you have more energy when you are exercising regularly. Start out by stretching for just a few minutes each day. Then try running in place or riding a stationary bike, perhaps while watching television. Begin slowly. You may need help to design a program that is right for you. Ask your gym teacher or school's coach how to get started. Or try one of the many exercise DVDs you can do at home.

Another excellent way to get exercise is to join a beginning exercise or dance class. Paying for a class will provide you with extra motivation to do your exercises on a regular basis. Also, being with other people who are just starting out will make you feel more comfortable. Sports can also provide you with strenuous physical activity if you enjoy competition. However, no amount of competitiveness is required to work on your body. It can be done with others or in private.

How much time should you exercise daily? Set a realistic goal, especially if you haven't been exercising regularly. Begin with five to ten minutes daily and over a few weeks. Doctors suggest that you build up to at least fifteen to twenty minutes of vigorous exercise daily. Or you could do thirty minutes of vigorous exercise every other day.

Most important, pick something you like to do. That way, you will have a better chance of staying with your program. Make exercise something you look forward to doing each day. Remember, though, to use moderation—compulsive exercise (sometimes called exercise addiction) is classified today as a serious eating disorder-related problem. Do not let exercise take over your life. It should not isolate you from you family or friends, and if it does become the single focus in your life, then it has become unhealthy for you.

EATING RIGHT—FOR LIFE

Changing any habit is hard work. It is especially hard if you try to make lots of changes at once. This is certainly true of developing new healthy eating habits. These are some of the strongest habits in your daily life.

Be patient with yourself. You'll still make some poor food choices. You'll overeat on occasion. You're human. Forgive yourself and get back into your diet plan.

No one has found an easy way to lose weight and keep it off. Weight loss is not a simple matter. You are not alone, however. There are many people willing to help you. There are organizations and support groups that can assist you, including Overeaters Anonymous, the American Obesity Association, the American Dietetic Association, and the National Eating Disorders Association, among many others.

There is no such thing as quick and easy weight loss. Keeping weight off after you lose it is even more challenging. But if you have faith in yourself and are willing to work hard, you can do anything you set your mind to. Sometimes you will give in to temptation and break your diet or skip your exercises. Sometimes you will feel like giving up. But if you keep trying, you will succeed. So get started—and remember, do it for yourself.

Glossary

adolescence The years that begin at puberty (about ages ten to twelve) and end when the body stops growing (about ages eighteen to twenty).

amphetamines Drugs that speed up the functions of the brain and body.

anorexia nervosa An eating disorder that results in severe weight loss; self-starvation.

bingeing Eating an unusually large amount of food in a short time.

bulimia An eating disorder that establishes a cycle of bingeing and purging.

calorie A unit of measure for the amount of energy our bodies get from food.

compulsive eater One who cannot resist eating.

diuretics Drugs that cause the body to eliminate water by increasing the flow of urine.

energy Body's ability to do work.

fad or crash diet A diet that promises quick weight loss by limiting the number of foods or food groups. A fad diet is usually only popular for a short period of time.

Glossary

fasting Not eating during a period of time.

laxatives Drugs that cause bowel movements.

metabolism The process by which all living things turn food into energy and living tissue.

obese Having excess body fat.

purging Getting rid of unwanted food by dangerous methods such as self-induced vomiting.

self-image How a person feels about herself or himself.

set-point The body's "natural" weight.

stress A physical, chemical, or emotional factor that causes tension in a person's body or mind.

Resources

American Dietetic Association Headquarters

120 South Riverside Plaza, Suite 208

Chicago, IL 60606-6995

(800) 877-1600

www.eatright.org

This organization offers information on food and nutrition for maintaining a healthy diet and can refer you to a registered dietitian or nutritionist in your area.

America on the Move Foundation

44 School Street, Suite 325

Boston, MA 02108

(800) 807-0077

www.americaonthemove.org

This organization provides information and assistance on healthy eating habits and physical activity.

Anorexia Nervosa and Related Eating Disorders, Inc.
   (ANRED)

P.O. Box 5102

Eugene, OR 97405

Resources

(503) 344-1144

www.anred.com

ANRED provides information about well-known eating disorders, including anorexia, bulimia, binge eating, and exercise addiction. It offers suggestions for self-help and important information about recovery and prevention of these disorders.

Centers for Disease Control and Prevention (CDC)

U.S. Department of Health and Human Services

1600 Clifton Road

Atlanta, GA 30333

(404) 639-3534

(800) 311-3435

www.cdc.gov

The CDC is the chief federal agency for protecting the health and safety of Americans. It provides information related to weight and health concerns and offers resource information and guidance regarding diet, nutrition, and the prevention of obesity.

Eating Disorder Awareness & Prevention, Inc. (EDAP)

603 Stewart Street, Suite 803

Seattle, WA 98101

(206) 382-3587

members.aol.com/edapinc

This organization strives to increase the awareness of eating disorders and provides information for those interested in learning about how to prevent them.

Eat Well and Keep Moving

Harvard School of Public Health

Department of Nutrition

665 Huntington Avenue, 2-253a

Boston, MA 02115

(617) 432-1086

www.hsph.harvard.edu/nutritionsource/EWKM.html

This organization provides an educational program for children to help them choose nutritious diets and physical activity for a healthy lifestyle.

Obsessive Compulsive Foundation

676 State Street

New Haven, CT 06511

(203) 401-2070

www.ocfoundation.org

This foundation offers information on obsessive-compulsive disorder and support groups.

WEB SITES

Due to the changing nature of Internet links, Rosen Publishing has developed an online list of Web sites related to the subject of this book. This site is updated regularly. Please use this link to access the list:

http://www.rosenlinks.com/dz/difa

For Further Reading

Bean, Anita. *Awesome Foods for Active Kids: The ABCs of Eating for Energy and Health*. Alameda, CA: Hunter House, 2006.

Bell, Julia. *Massive*. New York, NY: Simon Pulse, 2005.

D'Elgin, Tershia. *What Should I Eat? A Complete Guide to the New Pyramid*. New York, NY: Ballantine Books, 2005.

Diet Wars. WGBH Educational Foundation Frontline series video. 2004. www.pbs.org.

Ingram, Scott. *Want Fries with That? Obesity and the Supersizing of America* (Watts Library). New York, NY: Franklin Watts, 2005.

Jukes, Mavis, and Lilian Wai-Yin Cheung. *Be Healthy! It's a Girl Thing: Food, Fitness, and Feeling Great*. New York, NY: Crown Books for Young Readers, 2003.

Kay, Kathlyn. *Am I Fat? The Obesity Issue for Teens* (Issues in Focus Today). Berkeley Heights, NJ: Enslow Publishers, 2006.

Kirberger, Kimberly. *No Body's Perfect: Stories by Teens About Body Image, Self-Acceptance, and the Search for Identity*. New York, NY: Scholastic, 2003.

Danger Zone: Diet Fads

Mackler, Carolyn. *The Earth, My Butt, and Other Big Round Things*. Cambridge, MA: Candlewick, 2003.

McClure, Cynthia Rowland. *The Monster Within: Facing an Eating Disorder*. Grand Rapids, MI: Revell, 2002.

Owens, Peter. *Teens Health and Obesity* (The Gallup Youth Survey: Major Issues and Trends). Broomall, PA: Mason Crest Publishers, 2005.

Salmon, Margaret B. *Food Facts for Teenagers: A Guide to Good Nutrition for Teens and Preteens*. 2nd ed. Springfield, IL: Charles C. Thomas, 2003.

Schlosser, Eric. *Chew on This: Everything You Don't Want to Know About Fast Food*. Boston, MA: Houghton Mifflin, 2006.

Schroeder, Barbara, and Carrie Wiatt. *The Diet for Teenagers Only*. New York, NY: Regan Books, 2005.

Stinson, Kandi M. *Women and Dieting Culture: Inside a Commercial Weight Loss Group*. Piscataway, NJ: Rutgers University Press, 2001.

Stromberg, Gary, and Jane Merrill. *Feeding the Fame: Celebrities Tell Their Real-life Stories of Eating Disorders and Recovery*. Center City, MN: Hazelden Publishing and Educational Services, 2006.

Ward, Elizabeth M. *The Pocket Idiot's Guide to the New Food Pyramids*. New York, NY: Alpha, 2006.

Index

PHOTO CREDITS

Cover, pp. 1, 5 (middle), 9, 38 Shutterstock.com; p. 5 (top) © Mark Davis/ Getty Images; p. 5 (bottom) © Chris Hondros/Getty Images; p. 6 © Tim Boyle/Getty Images; p. 19 (top) www.istockphoto.com/Hasan Shaheed; p. 19 (middle) www.istockphoto.com/Bobbie Osborne; p. 19 (bottom) www.istockphoto.com/Ravet007; p. 23 © Andrew H. Walker/ Getty Images; p. 28 © Mario Tama/Getty Images; p. 33 www.istockphoto. com/Sean Locke; p. 47 (top) www.istockphoto.com/David Davis; p. 47 (middle) www.istockphoto. com/Suzannah Skelton; p. 47 (bottom) www. istockphoto.com/Jason Stitt; p. 51 © Getty Images.

Designer: Gene Mollica; Photo Researcher: Amy Feinberg